PUFFIN BOO

Sheltie: The Big Discovery

Make friends with

The little pony with the big heart

Sheltie is the lovable little Shetland pony with a big personality. His best friend and owner is Emma, and together they have lots of exciting adventures.

Share Sheltie and Emma's adventures in

SHELTIE THE SHETLAND PONY
SHELTIE SAVES THE DAY
SHELTIE AND THE RUNAWAY
SHELTIE FINDS A FRIEND
SHELTIE TO THE RESCUE
SHELTIE IN DANGER
SHELTIE RIDES TO WIN
SHELTIE AND THE SADDLE MYSTERY
SHELTIE LEADS THE WAY
SHELTIE THE HERO
SHELTIE IN TROUBLE
SHELTIE AND THE STRAY
SHELTIE AND THE SNOW PONY
SHELTIE ON PARADE
SHELTIE FOR EVER

♘

Peter Clover was born and went to school in London. He was a storyboard artist and illustrator before he began to put words to his pictures. He enjoys painting, travelling, cooking and keeping fit, and lives on the coast in Somerset.

Also by Peter Clover in Puffin

The Sheltie series

Sheltie
The Big Discovery

Peter Clover

PUFFIN BOOKS

Special thanks to Ann Ruffell
To Anna, Beth and Kathryn

PUFFIN BOOKS

Published by the Penguin Group
Penguin Books Ltd, 27 Wrights Lane, London W8 5TZ, England
Penguin Putnam Inc., 375 Hudson Street, New York, New York 10014, USA
Penguin Books Australia Ltd, Ringwood, Victoria, Australia
Penguin Books Canada Ltd, 10 Alcorn Avenue, Toronto, Ontario, Canada M4V 3B2
Penguin Books (NZ) Ltd, Private Bag 102902, NSMC, Auckland, New Zealand

On the World Wide Web at: www.penguin.com

Penguin Books Ltd, Registered Offices: Harmondsworth, Middlesex, England

First published 2000
1 3 5 7 9 10 8 6 4 2

Sheltie is a trademark owned by Working Partners Ltd
Copyright © Working Partners Ltd, 2000
All rights reserved

Created by Working Partners Ltd, London, W6 0QT

The moral right of the author has been asserted

Set in 14/22 Palatino

Made and printed in England by Clays Ltd, St Ives plc

British Library Cataloguing in Publication Data
A CIP catalogue record for this book is available from the British Library

ISBN 0–141–30800–1

Contents

The Prize
Painting

Chapter One

It was the first day of the Easter holidays and it was pouring with rain in Little Applewood. Emma rushed out of the house in her raincoat.

'Sorry I'm late, Sheltie,' she called to her little Shetland pony. 'I couldn't find my welly boots. You must be hungry.'

Sheltie shook his shaggy mane and droplets of water flew out in all directions. He pushed Emma aside to get to his breakfast and snorted into the manger. Bits of feed went all over the place.

'Sheltie, you're so greedy!' Emma giggled. Sheltie looked really funny with pony mix stuck to his wet mane.

'It's such horrible weather,' she sighed as she checked his hay rack. 'I was hoping to go out all day and have a picnic, but that wouldn't be much fun in the rain. Perhaps we ought to clean you up instead.' Sheltie's legs and hoofs were covered in sticky mud from his soggy paddock.

'Perhaps we'll go out with Sally and Minnow this afternoon – if the rain stops.' Minnow was Sheltie's best pony-friend. He was owned by Sally, Emma's best friend.

Sheltie blew a raspberry, and nearly puffed all the rest of his feed out of the manger.

'You just aren't going to behave yourself today, are you, Sheltie?' said Emma, laughing.

Mum had invited Sally over for lunch as it was still too wet for a picnic. Emma was in the middle of hosing down Sheltie's muddy legs when the little pony whinnied loudly and pulled at his tether rope. There was an answering whinny from the lane. In his excitement, Sheltie stamped on the end of the hose so that a jet of water spurted up all over Emma's face.

'Oh, Sheltie, you're so naughty!' spluttered Emma. 'Anyone would think you hadn't seen Minnow for ages.'

'What's going on?' called Sally with a laugh. She opened the paddock gate and led Minnow in.

Sheltie blew a raspberry and sprayed even more water from his wet muzzle. Sally jumped aside just in time.

'We're going to have lots of fun this holiday,' said Emma. She turned off the tap and coiled the hose neatly beside it.

'A whole two weeks to do what we like!' agreed Sally. She tucked Minnow's stirrups under his saddle and undid the girth strap. She lifted the saddle off and rested it on the top of the fence. Then she took off his bridle. Now Minnow could run about the paddock with

Sheltie and share the new spring grass with him.

The girls took Minnow's saddle into the tack room so that it didn't get any wetter, then went inside for lunch.

Mum had just finished baking a batch of her special chocolate brownies. '*After* lunch!' she said, laughing, as Emma's little brother, Joshua, stretched out his small hand for one. 'And then you can only have one each. These are for the antiques' fair on Saturday. I'm making a batch every day and putting them in the freezer.'

'We'd better keep them away from Sheltie,' said Emma, giggling. Sheltie had a very sweet tooth.

'Mum and Dad are going to bring lots of things to sell,' said Sally. 'I hope we make enough money to mend the church bell.'

Little Applewood's church bell was cracked, and made a very peculiar clanking noise instead of a proper ring. It was going to cost a lot of money to mend.

'It should certainly help the fund,' said Mum with a smile. 'I must look round the cottage to see if *we've* got anything that somebody might want to buy.'

At last the rain stopped. Emma and Sally tacked up their ponies for a ride.

'Where to?' asked Sally.

'We'll let Sheltie decide,' said Emma.

Emma held the reins loosely so that Sheltie could take up the lead. The little

Shetland pony tossed his mane and trotted off in front of Minnow. He loved rainy weather. It made the ground soft and easy to walk on. His short legs splashed through the puddles, sending up showers of spray.

Emma and Sally expected Sheltie to take the bridle path through Bramble Woods. There was plenty of space there for the ponies to canter. Or they thought he might lead them to the fields over towards Barrow Hill where they could have an energetic gallop.

But Sheltie took the road towards the village. Just as they reached the church, Sheltie stopped so suddenly that Minnow nearly barged into him. Emma kicked her heels, but Sheltie refused to budge.

'There's nothing special here, Sheltie,'
said Emma. 'Walk on.'

Sheltie did walk on, but instead of
going past the church he turned right,
through the gate and up the path to the
church door. He neighed softly and

pawed the gravel path with his hoof.

Sally giggled. 'It's not Sunday, Sheltie.'

Emma was curious. 'Why have you brought us here, Sheltie?' she said. She slid off Sheltie's back and handed the reins to Sally. Then she tried the latch and pushed at the door. It was unlocked. Someone was already inside.

'Hello?' she called into the dim church.

'Who's that?' came the vicar's voice.

'It's me, Emma.'

She heard sloshing noises coming towards her and opened the door wider to see a huge pool of water covering the church floor …

Chapter Two

'Hello, Emma. Hi, Sally,' said the vicar
as he appeared in the doorway with an
armful of hassocks. 'There's a big hole in
the roof. Rain has been pouring in all
morning!'

Sheltie clattered his hoofs and tried to
push his way past the vicar and into the
church. Luckily Sally was still holding
on to his reins.

'Wait a minute, Sheltie,' said Emma.

13

She took the reins from Sally and
tethered him loosely to a wooden seat
outside the church door. 'Can we help?'
she asked the vicar.

'I need to clear out everything that
might be damaged by the rain,' he said.
He put the hassocks down on the stone
bench in the porch. 'The rain has
stopped for now, at least, but we can't
risk putting anything back until the
roof is mended.' He looked up and
sighed.

'Is there a lot to move?' asked Emma.

The vicar nodded. 'The hole is in the
worst place possible. There are lots of
valuable things here. I'll have to take
them all over to the village hall for safe-
keeping. It's going to take all day!'

Sheltie nudged at Emma and neighed.

He pawed at the ground and tried again to move into the church, but his tether was too short. He twisted his fat little body round until his big shaggy head could reach the stone bench. Then he took hold of one of the hassocks with his teeth and pulled at it.

'Sheltie, what are you doing?' cried Emma. Then she stopped. 'I know, you want to help too.' She suddenly had an idea. 'If we brought Sheltie's little cart, *he* could take a lot of stuff over to the village hall.'

'And if you lend Minnow Sheltie's saddlebags, we could carry even more!' cried Sally.

'What a good idea!' said the vicar, laughing.

*

Emma and Sally came back with the
little fish cart and Sheltie's saddlebags.
The vicar had already brought the really
valuable things outside. There was a
silver cross and matching candlesticks,
and several silver cups.

'Those will tuck into the saddlebags

very nicely,' he said to Sally. 'If you wrap them up in this newspaper first, they won't bang against each other and get dented.' He went off to drag out the heavy cabinet that the silver was kept in. The cabinet was right underneath the leak. Its varnished wood was already spotted with rain.

'That will just fit into the fish cart,' said Emma. She helped him carry it outside.

After they had lifted it into the cart, the vicar looked up at the sky with a worried frown. 'It looks as if we're going to get another shower quite soon,' he said. 'Let's get this picture out next. It will be badly damaged if the rain gets to it.'

He had already unhooked it from its

place on the wall. Sally and Emma
helped him carry it out to the cart. It was
quite a boring picture, Emma thought.
Just a huge portrait of a cross-looking
man.

Sheltie and Minnow walked steadily
along the street towards the village hall.
They seemed to know they had to be
careful with the important things they
were carrying.

'Where shall we put these?' asked

Emma when they arrived. She panted as she tried to lift the heavy picture from the cart.

'Here – let me carry that,' said the vicar. 'We'll have to store everything right out of the way at the back because of the antiques' fair here on Saturday. What a time for the roof to spring a leak!'

Sheltie stood very still while the picture and the cabinet were unloaded.

Emma and Sally leaned the picture against the back wall of the hall.

'I wonder why they've kept this,' whispered Emma to Sally. 'I wouldn't want it hanging up in my house.'

Sally giggled. 'He does look rather grumpy, doesn't he? Perhaps he's an old vicar. Do you think ours will look grumpy too, when they do his portrait?'

The vicar didn't look grumpy now. He was looking very sad.

'Is there something else?' said Emma anxiously. 'Is anything damaged?'

The vicar smiled. 'No, thanks to you two – and Sheltie and Minnow, of course – I think we've saved everything,' he said. 'But I'm afraid our bell will have to wait even longer before it's repaired. We'll have to use the antiques' fair money to fix the roof instead. And I was really looking forward to having a bell again! Sunday doesn't seem like Sunday without it.'

On Saturday morning, Emma's family kitchen was very chaotic. Mum had been baking all week. So had a lot of other people in the village. There were boxes of cakes all over the kitchen table. Emma helped Dad load them into the boot of the car. Then she tacked Sheltie up and dashed inside to get Joshua.

'Come on, Joshua. There's no room for you in the car. We're going by pony!'

'Sheltie ride!' said Joshua, excited. He ran for his own small riding hat and jammed it on to his head.

As she led Sheltie and Joshua along the lanes to the village, Emma imagined she was helping a young prince to escape through the mountains, unselfishly giving up her own horse for him to ride.

Sally and Minnow were waiting for them outside the hall. Emma helped Joshua get down from Sheltie. The girls loosely tethered their ponies to a railing outside, at the back of the hall. Now they wouldn't be in the way of people bringing their antiques in to sell and to show the local experts who had been invited to the fair.

The morning was very busy. Emma helped Mum fill the big tea urn with water. Sally helped carry in the cakes from the car, and Joshua brought in a box of tea bags. Dad waited by the door to welcome the experts and look after them.

Mum's tea table was at the back, by a window. The painting they had rescued from the leaky church was leaning against the wall, underneath the window.

'Be careful you don't bang against it,' warned Mum. 'I don't suppose it's very valuable, but I wouldn't like anyone to spill tea over it.'

It was a bit of a squeeze behind the table. Emma and Sally set out cups and piled cakes on to plates.

'It's hot behind this urn,' said Mum. 'Let's have some fresh air.'

Emma pushed the window open and turned back to the table. 'Shall we put the prize cake in the middle?' she asked Mum. There was to be a raffle for the lovely chocolate cake that Mrs Linney had baked.

'What a good idea,' said Mum. 'Lots of people will see it and come to buy a ticket.'

All of a sudden, Emma felt someone blow hot air down her neck and nudge at her shoulder. She knew immediately

24

who it was. Her mischievous pony had
stuck his head through the window!

'No, Sheltie. Keep away from those
cakes!' scolded Emma.

But it was too late. Sheltie opened his
mouth and a pink iced fairy cake

disappeared inside it. Sally moved Mrs Linney's prize cake out of the way just in time!

Chapter Three

'You'll have to move Sheltie and
Minnow,' said Mum, emptying water
from the urn into the large teapot. 'It's
far too hot to shut the window.'

By now there were crowds of people
in the hall. Tables were filling up with
shiny vases, horse brasses, beautiful
boxes, silver teaspoons, old clocks and
all sorts of other things that the villagers
had found in their attics. There was a

table full of Victorian costumes, from hats to lace-trimmed nightdresses. Thirsty visitors crowded round Mum's refreshments table. Emma and Sally were too busy helping to move the ponies.

'We'll have to move the cake table forward instead,' gasped Sally, sloshing milk into the cups of tea.

'Excuse me,' said Emma to one of the antiques' experts queueing at the table. He was very tall with brown hair that flopped down over his eyes, and he looked strong enough to move tables. 'Could you help us move this out of the way of my pony?'

'Certainly,' said the expert, whose name was Mr Cooper. He helped Emma and Mum drag it forward so that Sheltie couldn't reach the cakes on top. 'Is he your art specialist?' he joked as Sheltie poked his fuzzy muzzle back through the window and nudged at the painting underneath it.

Emma laughed. 'He's a very clever pony,' she said, 'but I don't suppose he knows much about paintings. He's an expert on cakes though. Would you like one of these?'

'Yes, please,' said Mr Cooper. He drank his tea and ate one of Mum's special chocolate brownies before going off to look at Sally's mum's china.

The hall was getting more and more crowded and noisy. Everyone wanted the experts' advice about their favourite things. But Sheltie was only interested in the delicious cakes. Since the table had

been moved, he had only managed to
grab half a cheese scone that someone
had left on the window sill. He tried to
get more of his neck in, but his tether
rope wasn't quite long enough. Instead,
he kept banging his nose on to the
painting under the window. Each time,
it fell against Mum, or Emma, or Sally,
and they had to lean it back again.

Sheltie was very good for custom
though. Everyone wanted to buy a cup
of tea or a cake from a table with a
cheeky pony's head behind it!

'Emma, we'd better move that
painting,' said Mum, when Sheltie had
knocked it against her for the fourth
time. 'See if you can see Dad and ask
him to help.'

Emma searched the crowd for Dad. At

last she saw him with Mr Cooper. They
were pushing their way through the
crowd on their way to the tea table.

'We need your help, Dad,' said Emma.
'Can you move this painting somewhere
safe?'

'Does someone want an expert opinion on it?' asked Mr Cooper.

'Oh, no, it's nothing important,' said Emma. She explained about the leaky church roof and how they'd had to take everything to the village hall so that it didn't get damaged in the church. 'But there isn't much room here and Sheltie keeps knocking it over,' she said.

'I'll go and move Sheltie,' said Dad. 'That will be the best thing.'

Sheltie gave a huge snort and nudged at the picture with his nose. Mr Cooper laughed. 'I'll move the picture for you if you like. Is it valuable?'

'It's only a picture of a cross old vicar,' said Emma.

'No wonder he's cross, if he keeps

getting knocked over,' said Mr Cooper, laughing.

Then Sheltie shoved his nose so hard into the painting that it crashed to the ground.

'Oh, no!' Emma cried. 'Now the frame's coming off! Sheltie, look what you've done!'

She pushed Sheltie's fuzzy face back through the window.

As Mr Cooper dragged the painting out of the way of Mum's tea table, the frame and the backing fell off completely.

'Oh, look!' said Emma. 'There's another picture on the back of this one.'

She stood back to look at it. It wasn't another dark, boring portrait of a vicar. It glowed with colour. The people in the

picture looked happy and there were several children. But best of all, there were three horses – and a very small pony with a large head and melting brown eyes.

'It's lovely,' cried Emma. 'I think it's much nicer than the painting of the vicar. That pony looks just like Sheltie!'

'There you are. I think everything's safe now,' said Dad as he came back from moving the ponies. 'They're a good distance away.' He stopped and looked at the painting of the family with their horses. 'That's rather nice. Where did you find it?'

Emma explained while Mr Cooper bent down to look at it more closely. 'If I'm not mistaken, you may have something very good here,' he said, and fished a lens from his pocket. 'I wonder if it's signed?'

He focused the lens over the bottom right-hand corner of the painting. Then he grinned broadly at Emma.

'You're right. It is much nicer than the picture on the other side,' said Mr Cooper. 'This picture was painted by

Henry Butterworth. He was a very famous artist.'

'Famous?' gasped Sally.

'Yes, and discovering a lost painting by a famous artist is very exciting indeed,' said Mr Cooper. 'Lots of people will be interested in this.'

Emma beamed. 'And Sheltie discovered it!' she said. 'We'll have to hang it up somewhere so that everyone can see it properly.'

'Obviously it belongs to the church, but if they decide to sell it, one of the big London art galleries will probably be interested.' Mr Cooper smiled. 'Did you say this antiques' fair was in aid of your church bell fund?'

'It was,' said Emma. 'But now it's in aid of mending the roof.'

'Well, this could be the end of all your problems. If you sell it, you will have enough money to mend the roof *and* buy a brand new bell.'

Chapter Four

The following day, Mum invited Sally over for lunch. Afterwards, they were all going to go to the church, along with most of Little Applewood, to hear the vicar announce how much money they had raised at the antiques' fair. Emma was very excited because the vicar was also going to tell everyone about the painting Sheltie had discovered. Thanks to him, the church might have a new bell after all.

'The trouble is, the painting belongs to the church,' said Dad, helping himself to roast potatoes. 'All sorts of people have to be asked if it can be sold.'

'Yes,' agreed Mum, 'and although the money would be very useful, they might decide they want to keep the painting here in Little Applewood.'

'Maybe we should get Sheltie to nose around the rest of the church and see if he can find any more valuable paintings!' said Emma, her eyes shining.

At that moment, Sheltie came clattering in through the open kitchen door and made straight for the bowl of carrots on the table.

'Oh, dear. I don't think I locked the paddock gate properly,' said Sally, giggling.

Mum laughed. 'Paintings aren't the only things that Sheltie's good at nosing out!' she said.

Emma took Sheltie back to the paddock and made sure the little pin

was in place so that he couldn't slide the
bolt across again. She gave him a hug
and buried her face in his long mane.
'Just you wait, boy,' she said. 'When
everybody hears how clever you've
been, they'll all come and give you
carrots!'

But when they arrived at the church, it
seemed that most of the village had
heard about Sheltie's clever find
already.

'What a wonderful pony,' said
Marjorie Wallace, and gave Sheltie an
apple. She gave Minnow one as well, so
that he wouldn't feel left out.

'You're welcome to come to my house
and see what you can find,' said Mr
Crock, chuckling. He palmed Sheltie a

peppermint. Sheltie crunched it greedily and began to walk into the church porch. Minnow followed along behind.

'Hey! Those animals can't come inside,' Mr Crock said to Emma. He sounded severe, but there was a twinkle in his eye. He was very fond of Sheltie and Minnow really.

'They're allowed to today,' said Emma. 'The vicar invited us. It's important that Sheltie hears about what will happen to his picture.'

The girls tethered Sheltie and Minnow to a pillar at the back of the church. They both behaved beautifully while all the villagers piled in.

When everyone had arrived, the vicar came forward with a smile. First of all he thanked everyone for their help with the

antiques' fair, which had been a great
success and raised a lot of money.

'But as you all know, we have had
some problems with the church roof,'
the vicar went on. 'We've had it looked
at, and it will cost a great deal of money
to repair. We thought we would have to
use the money for the roof instead of for
the bell fund. But our bell's been saved
by a remarkable discovery …'

Sheltie gave a very loud whinny from
the back of the church, and everyone
laughed. Nearly all the village knew
what the vicar was going to say next,
but they wanted to hear it all the same.

'During the antiques' fair yesterday an
old painting was found,' said the vicar.
'The funny thing is that it's been
hanging in this church for years, but

nobody ever knew. On the back of one of our portraits of a past vicar of this church, there was another, much more valuable painting, by the famous artist Henry Butterworth. We've decided to sell it to a gallery in London, where everyone will be able to go and see it. Mr Cooper is certain that it is worth a great deal of money. So much money, in fact, that we will be able to pay for the roof and for a new bell!'

Everybody clapped and cheered.

'And this discovery is all thanks to a very special pony … Sheltie!'

Sheltie heard his name and gave a great snort. He tugged at his tether rope and pulled it away from the pillar. Then he trotted up the centre of the church, looking about him with great interest.

Emma dashed from her seat. 'Sheltie, you mustn't go up there.'

But Sheltie had already reached the area beneath the tower. Dangling down was a long, tasselled rope. He grabbed at it with his strong teeth. There was a

tinny, cracked sound from the top of the tower and everybody laughed.

The vicar grinned as well. 'Sheltie has just proved how much we need a new bell,' he said.

Dad's camera was at the ready. 'Here's another snap for the Sheltie story,' he said. 'Sheltie the bell-ringer!'

'Oh, Sheltie, you're so funny!' said Emma, laughing. 'And you're so clever!'

Sheltie's eyes twinkled as he stood with the end of the rope in his teeth. He yanked it again. As the echoes of the tinny clanking sound died away, he let go of the rope and blew a huge raspberry instead!

Duckling in Danger

Chapter One

'That was a lovely picnic,' said Sally as she and Emma rode home through Bramble Woods. The girls still had a week of their Easter holidays left, and they were determined to have lots of fun now that the sun was shining.

Sheltie tossed his mane and did a funny little dance at the edge of Prickly Thicket. He had certainly enjoyed the picnic – especially as Emma had asked

Mum to put an extra apple in for him.

'I feel very full,' said Sally.

'I'm full too,' said Emma. 'Let's stop by Horseshoe Pond and feed the remains of our picnic to the ducks. There might even be some baby ducklings.'

Sheltie whinnied and tossed his long mane. Emma knew he loved visiting the ducks. Emma's crusts sometimes missed the water and landed on the grass instead, and Sheltie always tried to grab them before the ducks did.

As they came out of Prickly Thicket, Emma urged Sheltie on. He gave a loud whinny and broke into a canter. Sally and Minnow followed, and the two girls and their ponies raced down the slope to the pond. Then Emma pulled on the reins.

'Slow down now, Sheltie. We don't want to frighten the ducks.'

Sheltie blew hard and slowed down to a trot.

'That's right. Nice and steady, boy,' said Sally to Minnow.

There were three pairs of mallard

ducks on the pond, and a pair of geese honking over on the far side, behind the big sycamore tree.

'Look, Sally!' said Emma excitedly. 'There are some ducklings. Aren't they cute?'

The ponies stood very still as the girls watched a family of five fluffy ducklings swim towards them. The little babies paddled frantically after their mother, waggling their tails in an effort to keep up.

Emma slid off Sheltie's back and took out the leftover sandwiches to throw to the ducklings. She gave Sally a handful of crusts and the girls threw small pieces of bread into the water.

All the ducks on the pond suddenly seemed to know there was food around.

They turned, almost at once, and swam towards Emma and Sally.

'Look at that one! Isn't he funny?' said Emma, laughing. She pointed to the last one of the family of five ducklings. He was the smallest of them all, and had to work even harder to keep up with his brothers and sisters.

'I love his tufty little head,' said Sally. She threw a piece of bread specially for

him, but one of the bigger ones turned quickly and grabbed it first.

'Greedy!' said Emma. She aimed the next piece of bread to drop right in front of the tufty-headed duckling's beak. This time, he managed to get a nibble before the rest of his family.

Sheltie walked softly up to the water's edge. He seemed very interested in the ducklings. He stood quite still while the mother duck clambered out of the water and walked right up to his hoofs. Her family came cheeping after her.

Sheltie lowered his shaggy head. Four of the ducklings scattered in alarm. But Tufty waddled right up to Sheltie's long mane. He cheeped loudly and pecked at the dangling strands of hair.

'He thinks your mane is something

good to eat, Sheltie,' said Emma. 'Isn't he funny?'

Then Tufty ran round Sheltie on his tiny webbed feet.

Emma was anxious. 'Be careful, Sheltie. He's right near your front hoof!'

Sheltie blew very gently, as if to tell Emma that he *was* being careful, and kept completely still until Tufty ran back to his mother.

'That's the last bit of bread,' said Sally, throwing her final crust far into the middle of the pond. There was a flash of green as two of the male ducks raced for it. The girls watched the ducks for a little while longer, then climbed back on their ponies, ready to go home.

'I wonder if Tufty will keep his little tuft, even when he's grown up?' said Emma.

Sheltie gave a whinny and began to walk slowly away from the pond. Both ponies would be ready for a nice meal of pony mix when they arrived back home.

Joshua was in the garden waiting for them as they clip-clopped along the lane by Emma's cottage. He clapped his hands as Emma bent to undo the paddock gate.

'Ducks!' he cried. 'Look! Ducks!'

'We've been to see the ducks, Joshua,' said Emma. 'But they're still on the pond. There are baby ones too. I'll take you to see them tomorrow.'

'Ducks,' said Joshua again, pointing.

Sally began to laugh. 'He's right, Emma,' she said. 'Look!'

Emma turned from closing the gate behind Sheltie and began to laugh too. Just behind her was a family of ducks. There was a mother and five ducklings. The last one had a funny little tuft on his head. They had followed Sheltie all the way back from the pond!

Chapter Two

'Oh, dear,' said Emma. 'What are we going to do? We don't have a pond here.'

She went inside to tell Mum while Sally loosely tethered Minnow to the fence.

'We'd better take them back to the pond straight away,' said Mum. 'I wonder how we could carry them.'

Joshua bent down to play with the

baby ducks, who didn't seem at all worried about being out in the big wide world.

Sheltie leaned his head over the paddock gate to say hello to the ducklings. Tufty scurried under the gate and played by Sheltie's hoofs, just as he had done by the pond. The little pony lifted his head gently so as not to startle the fluffy baby and turned towards his saddlebags. He nibbled at one of them, then nudged Emma.

'I can't take your saddlebags off just yet, Sheltie,' said Emma, worried. 'We have to think of a way to get these ducks back to their pond first.'

'I've got a basket, but it doesn't have a lid,' said Mum. 'I'll have to think of some way of covering it.'

She picked up one of the ducklings and showed Joshua how to cup it in his little hands.

Sheltie gave a quiet snort. Tufty had folded his wings and was squatting right beside one of Sheltie's hoofs.

'Cheep!' peeped the duckling.

His mother quacked and waddled under the paddock gate to her smallest baby. She prodded him and pushed him towards the gate. Tufty didn't like this at all, and kept trying to run back to Sheltie.

'I think you've made a friend, Sheltie,' said Sally.

Sheltie still wouldn't leave his saddlebags alone. He kept turning his head and nibbling at them. As soon as the mother duck had taken Tufty under

her wing, he blew a loud raspberry at
Emma.

'Are you trying to tell me you can
carry the ducks in your saddlebags?'
said Emma. 'Of course! Why didn't I
think of that?'

'What a good idea! Well done, Sheltie!'
said Mum. She bent down to cup one of
the ducklings in her hand. 'Come on,
little one. You're going for a nice ride
back home.'

Joshua thought this was great fun and
helped by catching a baby duck. Soon
they were all cheeping noisily in one of
Sheltie's saddlebags.

'But what about their mother?' said
Sally anxiously. 'I don't think she'll like
being carried in a saddlebag. I hope she
doesn't get lost on the way back.'

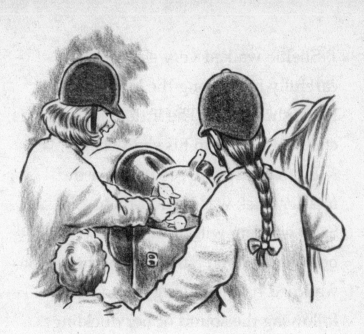

'Let's see what happens,' said Mum. 'I
think she'll probably follow her brood if
Sheltie walks very slowly. Why don't
you walk behind to make sure she goes
in the right direction?'

So Emma undid the paddock gate and
let Sheltie out again. She decided not to
ride him in case she squashed the
ducklings with her knees.

Sheltie walked very slowly and carefully back along the lane towards Horseshoe Pond. The little ducklings cheeped noisily in his saddlebag.

Emma turned to see whether the mother duck was behind them. She saw Sally walking with Minnow, and between her and Sally, the mother duck waddled happily along the road, following the sound of her ducklings!

When they arrived at the pond, the rest of the ducks came rushing up for more food.

'I think they must have liked our sandwiches,' said Sally.

'Especially these greedy ones here,' said Emma, laughing. She carefully lifted the ducklings out of Sheltie's saddlebag, one by one, and put them down on the ground. They rushed to their mother, who quacked loudly and hustled them into the pond.

'I don't think they're greedy,' said Sally, taking a carrot out of her bag for Minnow. 'I think they were following Sheltie. Look! Little Tufty has made great friends with him.'

The smallest duckling hadn't followed the rest of his family into the water. He waddled around Sheltie's hoofs, cheeping softly. Once again, Sheltie stood very quiet and still, and watched the fluffy baby with his intelligent brown eyes.

'Come on, Tufty,' said Emma. 'We have to go home and you have to go back to your family.'

Emma picked him up and reached out

over the water. She lowered him in carefully, just at the end of the line of his brothers and sisters. Tufty waggled his tiny tail, then paddled off after his family. But before Emma could climb back into his saddle, Sheltie blew a loud, rude raspberry, snatched the carrot out of Sally's hand and darted away.

'Hey, Sheltie! That's for Minnow!' cried Sally. Sheltie stopped just out of her reach and looked back at her with a twinkle in his eye. Then he broke into a canter and dashed off to the other side of Horseshoe Pond, sending his saddlebags flying off behind him.

Emma rushed after him, scattering some ducks by the side of the pond.

Sally jumped on to Minnow's back and turned him to try and head Sheltie off. But the little Shetland pony was ready for them. He was having a lovely game! He tossed his mane and whinnied loudly before charging off past Emma.

Emma just managed to catch hold of his reins. She skidded on the muddy ground where the ducks had been, but hung on stubbornly.

Suddenly Sheltie came to a stop and

Emma crashed into his side. She fell face down in the green slimy muck.

Sally giggled. She got off Minnow and managed to hold on to both ponies while Emma cleaned up her face.

'You did look funny!' said Sally.

'I'll give him funny!' said Emma. 'No peppermints for you tonight, boy!'

'I wish I'd brought my new camera,' said Sally. 'That would have made a brilliant photo!'

Chapter Three

Two days later, Emma rode out to the
pond again so that Sheltie could say
hello to his favourite duckling.

'That's funny, Sheltie. I can't see him.'

Sheltie snorted and shook his mane so
that his bridle jingled.

'I'm sure that was the mother duck – I
remember that mark on her beak. But
she only has four babies with her.
Maybe it's not that one after all.'

Just to make sure, Emma rode Sheltie slowly right round the pond. When they were back where they started, Sheltie whickered softly at the duck with the mark on its beak.

'You think that's the mother duck too, don't you, Sheltie?' said Emma. 'I wonder where Tufty's gone. I hope nothing bad's happened. We'll go and meet Sally and then come back and have another look.'

Sheltie seemed to think that was a good idea. He walked on as soon as Emma told him to.

They had only gone a little way towards Fox Hall Manor, where Sally lived, when Emma saw Mr Brown walking along the road towards Horseshoe Pond. Emma and Sheltie stopped to talk to him. She told him about the family of ducklings who followed Sheltie home.

Mr Brown laughed. 'I'm surprised the mother followed you,' he said. 'But baby ducks and geese often do take a fancy to people – or animals – and start thinking *they* are their mothers instead. Those little ones must have taken a liking to your Sheltie!'

Sheltie blew noisily and stamped his feet. That wasn't surprising, he seemed to say, because everybody took a liking to him!

'All right, Sheltie, we know you're wonderful,' said Mr Brown, with a chuckle.

'The duckling that liked Sheltie the most doesn't seem to be there today, though,' Emma told him. 'It was the smallest and he had a kind of tuft on the top of his tiny head.'

'Are you sure you've got the right mother duck?' asked Mr Brown.

'I'm quite sure,' said Emma, and told him about the mark on her beak.

Mr Brown looked grave. 'I shouldn't count on finding it, Emma,' he said. 'Not all ducklings survive to be grown up. All sorts of things can happen to them – especially if they're a little weaker. You say it was smaller than its four brothers and sisters?'

Emma nodded.

'Then I should think something's taken it. Probably a fox. There are a number of foxes around here.'

Emma felt quite miserable as she rode to Sally's house. Sheltie didn't help matters by stopping abruptly by a hawthorn tree in the hedge and refusing to walk on. Emma tried to pull him away, but he pushed his nose down into the thick, long grass under the hedge. He sniffled and then sneezed. Emma knew he always sneezed when he found mushrooms.

'Come away from there, Sheltie. They might be poisonous,' she warned, and she pulled at the reins to tell him to lift his head.

Sheltie pawed the ground and blew through his lips. Normally Emma would have slid off Sheltie's back to have a look at what he had found, but today she desperately wanted to see Sally and share her sadness about the little duckling.

'Sorry, Sheltie. Perhaps we'll look at what you've found on the way back. Walk on, please.'

Emma kept thinking about the poor little duckling being snatched by a fox.

By the time she got to Sally's, she was really upset. Sheltie pushed his soft muzzle into her neck as soon as she had dismounted and blew warm air in her ear.

Emma hugged him. 'You're so kind, Sheltie,' she whispered. 'But he was *your* favourite duckling too. I hope you don't understand what could have happened to him.'

'What's the matter, Emma?' said Sally when she saw Emma's sad face.

Emma told her about the missing duckling and what Mr Brown had said.

'Let's go back and see,' said Sally sensibly. 'Perhaps he was only hiding in the weeds at the edge. We'll probably find him waggling his little tail at the end of the line as usual. I've remembered my camera. When we see him, I'll take a picture.'

Emma cheered up a bit. 'I hope you're right,' she said. 'But I can't help feeling we ought to have gone to look at him yesterday.'

On the way back to Horseshoe Pond, Sheltie stopped at the same hawthorn tree in the hedge.

'Come on, Sheltie!' said Emma impatiently, pulling at the reins. 'They're only mushrooms, and we are not allowed to pick them.'

But this time Sheltie wouldn't take any notice of Emma. He stood there stubbornly, stamping on the ground and blowing great snorts.

'What's the matter with Sheltie?' said Sally. She slid down from her saddle and

went over to the hedge to have a look. 'I
can't see anything here,' she said.

Emma dismounted too. 'What is it,
Sheltie?' she said gently. Sheltie didn't
usually insist unless there was
something very important for her to see.

Sheltie pushed his nose further into
the hedge, blowing and puffing. Emma
drew back the tangled branches to have

a look. Suddenly she heard something. A tiny peeping sound. Emma tried to get further into the hedge, but the springy branches held her back. She tried crawling underneath them, and then she saw it.

Just where the cheeping noise was coming from, there was a hole. It looked like an old rabbit hole.

'There's a little bird down there,' she said to Sally. 'I'm going to try and get it out.'

'I wonder how it got there,' said Sally. 'Birds don't usually get stuck in rabbit holes. Perhaps it fell out of its nest in the hedge.' She searched in the hedge, but there didn't seem to be a nest anywhere above the rabbit hole.

'I can see it – just,' said Emma excitedly. 'And I'm sure I saw a flash of yellow too. Sally, I think it could be Tufty!'

Chapter Four

Emma could just see the little duckling's yellow downy feathers, but her arm wasn't quite long enough to reach down to where it was stuck.

'You try, Sally,' she said desperately. 'Your arm might be a bit longer than mine.'

But Sally's arm wasn't long enough either.

'Stay here, just in case a dog comes by,

or a fox,' said Emma, suddenly making up her mind. 'I won't be long. I'm going home to ask Mum or Dad to help.'

'I'll keep trying to reach him,' said Sally.

As she rode along the lane, Emma remembered that Dad wouldn't be home from work yet. But perhaps Mum's arm would be long enough to reach down into the old rabbit hole.

Emma's next-door neighbour, Mr Crock, was in his garden, watering a neat row of early cabbage seedlings. 'Is anything the matter, Emma?' he asked. 'You look worried.'

As Emma explained about the duckling in the rabbit hole, Sheltie pushed his nose over Mr Crock's garden

wall and managed to grab hold of the
handle of his watering can.

'Now then,' said Mr Crock. 'Just you
leave that alone.'

There was a twinkle in Sheltie's eye as
he yanked the watering can over the wall
and began trotting away with it.

'Come back, you wretched animal!'
yelled Mr Crock, running into the lane.
'Bring me back my watering can!'

'Sheltie!' Emma scolded, chasing after
him. 'You cheeky –' But then she
stopped. Her clever pony probably had
a very good reason for stealing the
watering can, and she had just guessed
what that reason might be.

'Sheltie, I know!' she cried. 'If we pour
water into the rabbit hole, perhaps the
duckling will be able to float up to the

top of the hole. Then we'll be able to reach him.'

'Humph,' said Mr Crock, when Emma explained why she thought Sheltie had made off with his watering can. 'That's all very well, but he ought to ask properly first.' Then his eyes twinkled at

Emma. 'That pony of yours is too clever by half!' he said.

Sheltie tried to blow a raspberry, but the watering-can handle was in his mouth. He dropped it, and blew a really loud raspberry at Mr Crock.

'There's no need to be rude,' said Emma, trying not to laugh.

Mr Crock took the can and went back into his garden to fill it under the tap. 'Here you are. But bring it back when you've finished with it,' he said.

Emma promised she would. She balanced the full can carefully in front of her on Sheltie's saddle and told her pony to walk on. Sheltie walked steadily, as if he knew he had an awkward cargo on his back.

'Sheltie had a wonderful idea,' said

Emma, when they reached Sally and Minnow. 'Can you take this can?'

Sally helped her lift the heavy can down from the saddle.

'What do we want it for?' she said, puzzled.

'Wait and see,' said Emma. She crawled under the hedge to the rabbit hole, where little Tufty was still cheeping loudly. 'It's all right, Tufty. We're going to save you.'

Gently and carefully, she poured some water into the hole and held her breath. Would it fill up, or would the water just soak into the ground?

The duckling *did* look a bit closer to the top. Emma poured a little more water in. Tufty sounded very excited and cheeped madly, and behind her

Sheltie whickered, as if to encourage his tiny friend.

But then it seemed as if the little duckling was right down at the bottom of the hole again. Emma was disappointed. It hadn't worked. The water had all seeped away.

Emma had another idea. If she poured the water in quickly, the little duckling might float far enough up for Sally to catch hold of it. She told Sally her plan.

Emma then took a deep breath, and, carefully but quickly, poured all the rest of the water from the can down the side of the hole.

It worked! She could see Tufty's funny little feathery head rising towards them.

'Quick, grab him, Sally!' she gasped.

Sally put out her hands and caught the

duckling, just in time before the water began to sink down into the earth.

Sheltie whinnied with excitement. He pushed his floppy forelock forward eagerly and blew gently on the duckling with his soft lips.

'It's Tufty! It's your little friend, Sheltie,' cried Emma.

'And aren't you the cleverest pony in the world to work out how to rescue him!' said Sally. She cradled the little duckling in her hands.

'Let's take Tufty straight back to his family,' said Emma. 'Here, Sheltie, you can give him a ride.'

Very gently, she perched Tufty on Sheltie's head.

'Hold it there!' said Sally. She raised her camera.

CLICK!

After a few seconds, Sally took hold of the square of paper which came out of the camera. The girls watched as the picture slowly developed. First they could see Sheltie's shape, then the

yellow duckling nestling on his shaggy head.

'Don't they look funny together?' said Emma. 'What a great picture!'

Sheltie snorted and whinnied – very quietly so that he did not frighten his

passenger. But it was enough to tell
them how proud he was of his brilliant
rescue!

Flower Power

Chapter One

Emma hummed as she filled Sheltie's hay rack. Sheltie shifted his hoofs on the straw-covered floor and moved closer to Emma. She could feel his warm breath on her cheek. He pushed his soft muzzle into her side, trying to find the pocket which held his morning carrot treat.

'Sheltie, you're so gorgeous!' she said, and threw her arms round his neck. 'But

I know exactly what you're looking for! Just wait till I've done this.'

She finished filling the rack, then took the carrot out of her pocket, broke it into two pieces, and palmed him one of them.

'You'll enjoy today,' she told him. 'We're going to Hawthorn Copse for the last picnic of our holidays. Sally and I are back at school next week, so it's a special treat for you and Minnow.'

Sheltie snorted and pushed at her for the second half of his carrot.

'Don't worry, I'll get Mum to put an extra apple in our picnic for you,' she promised. 'Now I'm going to get my breakfast and then we'll go and call on Sally and Minnow.'

Emma sang all the way back across

the paddock and up the little path to the back door.

'You're in a good mood today,' said Dad, yawning as he laid the table for breakfast, still in his pyjamas.

'It's a lovely sunny day,' said Emma, 'so we're going to Hawthorn Copse for a picnic.'

She hugged Joshua, who was waiting for his breakfast, and reached for her own bowl of cereal.

'I wish I was going to Hawthorn Copse instead of to work,' said Dad. 'I'd better get dressed, I suppose.'

'I'd bring Joshua and come too,' said Mum, 'only I've a meeting about this year's summer fête programme.' She spread out the morning paper on the table. 'Oh, look. There's something about Hawthorn Copse here.'

Emma poured milk on her cereal. 'What does it say?' she said eagerly.

'Oh, dear,' said Mum. 'Listen to this.' She read from the paper: '*At the beginning of next week, Dillon and Jones, Architects and Builders, will be making a start on clearing the site for a development of fifty new homes.*'

Emma stopped with her spoon half-way to her mouth. 'The site? Do they mean Hawthorn Copse?'

'I'm afraid they do, Emma,' said Mum. 'You'd better make the most of your favourite picnic place, because from next week, it won't be there any more.'

Emma was very upset. 'But they can't do that!' she said. 'It's a beautiful place!

It will be awful if they cut the trees down and put up horrible new houses instead!'

'There's nothing we can do to stop them, Emma,' said Dad. 'But they won't be horrible houses. Dillon and Jones design really smart houses. And I don't suppose they'll cut down all the trees – only the ones which will get in the way of the buildings.'

'Even nice houses won't look as lovely

as Hawthorn Copse!' said Emma stubbornly. 'There are plenty of other places where they could build houses. There are fields and fields out there!' She waved her arm excitedly and nearly knocked over the milk jug.

'But the fields are good farming land, Emma,' said Mum. 'People need food as well. They can't build on farm land.'

'I'd rather starve!' said Emma crossly. She knew she was being unreasonable, but she thought anyone who wanted to build houses on her favourite spot was unreasonable too. She raced out of the house to tell Sheltie.

Sheltie seemed to know Emma was upset. He whickered softly, and rubbed his soft muzzle over her worried face. Emma cuddled him and kissed him on the nose. 'This is something even you can't help with, Sheltie, however clever you might be,' she told him. 'Let's go and get Sally quickly. We've got to make the most of today. It might be the last picnic we ever have in Hawthorn Copse.'

The grass was velvety smooth in the glade in the middle of the little copse of trees. There were wild flowers beside the bridle path that wound through the copse, and more flowers further into the trees.

'How can people cut this down?' said Sally. 'What a good thing I've remembered my camera. I'll take lots of pictures so at least we'll be able to remember it.'

'It won't be the same though,' said Emma with a sigh.

Sheltie shook his head so hard that his bridle jingled. He lifted his head and took a great sniff of the air. Then he pawed the ground, as if to make sure he too would remember what it felt like. Emma tethered him loosely to a tree near their picnic spot. Sally tethered Minnow next to him. There was a clump of juicy grass for them to graze on. Emma and Sally had decided to visit all their favourite places before they ate their sandwiches.

Suddenly Sheltie whickered, and pulled at his tether rope.

'We won't be long, Sheltie,' said Emma, giving him a hug. 'Stay with Minnow and keep him company.'

But Sheltie stamped his feet and yanked at his rope. His ears went flat.

'What is it, Sheltie?' asked Emma.

Then suddenly she heard the crackling of a twig behind her. Emma turned round to see two men wearing bright green jackets and carrying strange instruments.

'What are *they* doing?' asked Emma.

Chapter Two

The two men were wandering about in a fenced-off area. The taller man had blond hair and freckles, and was carrying a three-legged stand which he stuck into the ground. The other, shorter man had dark curly hair and a beard. He was holding up a red and white striped stick, some way away from his companion.

'OK, ready,' shouted the tall man. He

bent down to peer through what looked
like a very small telescope at the top of
his tripod.

When he straightened up, the shorter,
bearded man picked up his red and
white striped stick and moved away
from him. 'OK, Dave?' he shouted.

'OK, Jim!' replied Dave. And he

looked through his telescope again.

'What are you doing?' called Emma curiously.

The men explained that they were surveying the land for the new housing development. 'We have to find out where all the bumps and hollows are before we start work,' said Jim.

Sheltie was curious too. He pulled at his tether rope and walked towards the fence. The rope was just long enough. If he stuck his neck right out, he could reach Dave's green jacket. He nudged at Dave and breathed hot breath into his ear.

Dave jumped. 'Hey, don't let that animal eat my gear.'

'It's all right,' said Emma, laughing. 'He only wants to see if there's

something to eat in your pocket. He
likes peppermints.'

'Oh, that's good,' said Dave. He fished
out a roll of peppermints from his
pocket and let Emma show him how to
palm one for Sheltie.

The little Shetland pony sniffed at it
and blew a rather rude raspberry at
Dave.

'Go on, Sheltie,' urged Emma. 'Take it.
It's all right.'

Sheltie blew noisily over Dave's hand
and puffed the peppermint off his palm.

'Sheltie, you're being very naughty,'
said Emma. 'Try again,' she told Dave.

'He's quite a comic little fellow, isn't
he?' said Dave. 'Hey, Jim – see if you can
do better.'

Sheltie didn't want a peppermint from

Jim's palm either. Dave offered one to
Minnow to see if he had better manners.
Minnow took the peppermint gently.
Sally grinned. 'Sheltie must be saving up
his appetite for our picnic,' she said.

It was still too early to eat lunch, so
Emma and Sally wandered around,

looking at their favourite places for the last time. They had decided to untether their ponies, and Sheltie and Minnow walked along next to them. Sheltie stopped at a bramble thicket and pushed his nose in. Sally looked to see what he had found.

'Look, Emma,' said Sally. She pointed to a small purple flower in the thicket. 'Isn't it lovely!'

Emma peered closely at it. 'I've never seen one of those before,' she said.

'Shall we pick it and take it home?' suggested Sally. 'We could look it up in your mum's wild flower book.'

'Good idea,' said Emma. Then she remembered. 'No, we mustn't. Wild flowers should be left alone for everyone to enjoy. But we could take a photograph of it with your camera.'

'What a brilliant idea,' said Sally. She focused carefully and pressed the button. *CLICK!* After a moment the stiff paper slid out from the camera and they watched their flower begin to take shape.

'That's really good,' said Emma.

The men on the other side of the fence were watching them with interest.

'That's a smart camera,' said Dave. 'What are you taking pictures of?'

Sally and Emma took the developing picture over to the fence.

'It's a beautiful flower. We've never seen one like it before,' said Emma. 'Look.'

The two men glanced at each other, then back at the picture. 'I think it's

quite common,' said Jim. 'But you're right. It's very pretty.'

When Emma arrived home, Sheltie made straight for his water trough. He had a long drink, then Emma took off his tack and hung the saddle on the fence.

'It was a lovely day, wasn't it, Sheltie?'

she said as she gave him a quick brush down. 'I can't believe we won't be able to picnic there any more.'

Sheltie blew a loud raspberry and looked at her with a twinkle in his eye.

'No, Sheltie,' sighed Emma. 'I really don't think you'll be able to do anything to help. It would be wonderful if you could, but I can't see any way of stopping them building their nasty houses.'

After Emma had put Sheltie's tack away and had given him his evening meal of pony mix, she went inside to tell Mum and Dad about the lovely flower Sheltie had found.

'Sounds like an orchid to me,' said Dad.

Emma thought of the big, beautiful

flowers that Dad sometimes bought for Mum on special occasions. 'No, it wasn't anything like that,' she said. 'It was quite small. About the size of a bluebell.'

'Wild orchids which grow in this country are quite small,' said Dad. 'Let's get out Mum's book of wild flowers and see if you recognize it.'

Dad was right. It *was* an orchid. Emma pointed her finger at the page. 'It was one of those,' she said.

'*A Military orchid*,' read Dad. 'Are you sure, Emma? It says they're very rare. Could it have been one of these? A Green-winged orchid? It looks almost the same, and it's quite common.'

Emma looked closely at the pictures. 'I'm sure it was that one,' she said, pointing again to the picture of the

Military orchid. 'It wasn't quite as dark a colour as that other one. But Sally took a photograph of it, so we can match it up with the picture in the book.'

'Phone her now,' said Dad, 'and ask her to bring the photo when she comes over tomorrow.' He sounded quite excited. 'If you're right, then I think we might just be able to stop that development in Hawthorn Copse.'

Chapter Three

Sally promised to come over early,
before Dad left for work, and to bring
the photograph with her. Dad was
outside the house, waiting for Sally and
Minnow to arrive, even before Emma
had finished grooming Sheltie.

Sheltie suddenly whinnied. A moment
later, Emma heard Minnow's hoofs
clattering down the lane.

'Sorry, Sheltie, I'll have to finish you

later,' she said, throwing the dandy brush into her grooming-kit box. 'Dad seems to think this flower is important. Don't get yourself dirty again, will you?'

Sheltie looked at her with a twinkle in his eye, rushed off to a muddy patch by the fence and began stomping around in it.

But for once Emma wasn't looking. She raced to the gate and climbed over it.

Sally was startled to see Emma's dad waiting for her too. She waved an envelope as Minnow trotted round the corner along the little path which led to the paddock.

'Here it is,' she said, and handed Dad the envelope.

'Tether Minnow to the fence,' said Dad in a hurry, 'and let's go inside to see

whether Emma's right about your
flower.'

The book was open on the kitchen
table. Sally had taken a very good
picture of the purple flower. Dad put it

against the book's picture of a Military orchid, and then against the Green-winged orchid that looked a bit like it.

'I do believe you're right, Emma,' he said with a broad grin. 'Well done, flower detective! I must go to work now, but I'll come home early and we'll go up to the copse and have a proper look at your special plant.'

'What's so special about it?' demanded Sally. 'I know it's very pretty, but so are lots of other flowers.'

'It's very rare,' said Emma importantly.

'Not only rare, but protected by law,' said Dad. 'Once we tell the council, they may have to stop the site being developed. Nobody is allowed to dig up rare plants!'

Emma remembered how nearly they had picked it. It was really lucky they had decided to take a photo of it instead. 'We could take pictures of all sorts of flowers today,' she said. 'We might even find something so rare that nobody's ever seen one before. Then we can really make sure that no one builds anything on Hawthorn Copse.'

'I'm going to take a picture of Sheltie first,' said Sally.

Emma beamed. 'What a good idea,' she said. 'But I haven't finished grooming him yet. Wait until he looks clean and tidy.'

Dad honked the car horn to tell them he was leaving for work and Mum brought Joshua out to wave to him. Sheltie whinnied goodbye too.

'Oh, Sheltie, what have you been doing?' cried Emma.

The little Shetland pony's legs were covered in thick, sticky mud. He blew a loud raspberry at her.

'That will make a really good picture!' said Sally with a grin. She lifted the camera. *CLICK!*

Mum laughed. 'Look, Joshua. Watch Sheltie grow on the paper.'

Joshua watched the picture of Sheltie slowly appear on the photographic paper. 'Sheltie!' he cried, and clapped his hands.

After Sally had taken pictures of Mum and Joshua, the girls went to clean Sheltie again and tack him up for their morning ride across the downs.

As they rode, Emma imagined that

she and Sally were explorers on an expedition to look for rare plants. She stared keenly into the bushes. Sheltie snuffled into the hedgerows, just as if he was searching too.

But though they found a few wild flowers, there were none that they had never seen before.

Dad came home early and Emma and Sally walked their ponies with him to Hawthorn Copse.

The two surveyors were still there. Dad went across to the fenced-off area and called to them. Dave and Jim came over to the fence. Sheltie snorted and pawed the ground.

'Hush, Sheltie,' said Emma. 'This is important business.'

Sheltie tossed his head and blew noisily. Minnow snorted too.

'Does he want another peppermint?' asked Dave, grinning. 'I've got the rest of that packet here.'

He pulled out the packet of peppermints and tried to palm one to Sheltie. But the little Shetland pony tossed his mane and showed his teeth.

'Sheltie, stop being so rude,' said Emma. She turned him round so that he couldn't see the men. 'And be quiet. Dad has some important things to say.'

'I'm sorry, lads, but you may have to stop surveying here,' said Dad.

'How's that?' said Jim. He glanced at Dave.

'There's a rare and protected plant growing here,' explained Dad. 'A

Military orchid. I'm going to have to tell the council about it.'

'What plant?' said Dave. 'We don't know anything about a plant.'

'It was the one we showed you a picture of yesterday,' said Emma. 'Don't you remember?'

'I took a photograph of it with my new camera,' said Sally. She showed them her camera to remind them.

'Oh, that,' said Jim. 'We had a look, yes. But it was quite a common one. You can't stop progress for a common flower.'

'Let's go and find it, shall we?' said Dad politely. 'Do you remember exactly where it was, Emma?'

'Sheltie knows,' said Emma confidently. 'Don't you, boy? It's quite near the fence, by a bramble thicket.'

121

The men jumped over the fence and followed them. They looked a bit worried.

'I didn't realize there were so many bramble thickets,' whispered Sally to Emma as they searched through the copse. 'I can't remember which one it was.'

'Well, Emma?' said Dad. 'Are we getting close?'

Emma looked around her. If they couldn't find the Military orchid, they wouldn't be able to stop the developers. They simply *had* to find it! 'I think so,' she said.

'I'm sure we've come too far,' said Jim. 'There was a kind of hollow log near your plant, and I think we passed that a few minutes ago.'

'I don't remember a hollow log,' said Emma. 'Do you, Sally?'

Sally frowned. 'I'm not sure,' she said.

'Better go back again,' said Dad.

But Sheltie didn't want to be turned round. He pushed his front hoofs firmly into the soft ground, threw back his head and whinnied loudly. When Emma tried to turn him, he nudged into her and pushed in the other direction.

'Come on, Sheltie!' said Emma in despair. 'Look – Minnow's behaving beautifully. Why can't you?'

Sheltie gave a huge snort and pulled away from her.

'I wonder …' said Dad. 'Let him go where he wants, Emma. You've always said he's a clever little pony. Let him show us how clever he can be.'

'Clever!' said Dave with a laugh.
'Horses aren't clever.'

'He's not a horse,' said Emma. 'He's a
Shetland pony. And he is *very* clever.'

Sheltie blew a loud raspberry.

'Come on, Sheltie,' Emma whispered to

him. 'You know where to go.' She made an encouraging click with her tongue and patted him on his hairy flank.

Sheltie stepped out confidently. He took great sniffs of the air, as if he were smelling it for special flower scents.

'Oh, look!' said Emma. 'There's a hoof print.'

In the soft ground was a clear print of one of Sheltie's shoes.

'And here's another,' said Sally. 'That proves it. We must have come this way yesterday.'

'Yes, but you were all over the place yesterday,' said Jim quickly. 'I still think you've come too far.'

Sheltie lifted his head and gave a soft whinny. Then he bent his head.

'That's the place!' said Emma

excitedly. 'Look – there's Sheltie's hoof print right by those brambles.'

'But where's the flower?' said Dad. 'I can't see it.'

'I told you,' snapped Dave. 'You're looking in the wrong place.'

'And it wasn't one of those whatever you said it was,' added Jim. 'I've seen loads of these flowers. They're really common. Sorry, but there you are.'

'Better get back to work,' said Dave. 'We've still got a bit to do before it gets dark.'

They turned and went back to where they had been surveying.

'It *was* here. I know it was here!' said Emma in despair. 'It had thick leaves at the bottom. Look – these must be the leaves.'

Emma reached down, suddenly excited. But inside the little fan of leaves was a broken-off stalk …

Chapter Four

'Look at that!' cried Sally. 'Somebody's picked it!'

'Do you think it was those men?' said Emma. 'I bet they knew it was here and were just trying to pretend it wasn't.'

'It might not have been them,' said Dad. 'Quite a lot of people come to Hawthorn Copse. Not everyone realizes that you shouldn't pick wild flowers.' But he looked quite upset too.

'And I let them give Sheltie a peppermint!' said Emma crossly.

'But he didn't want to take it from them,' Sally pointed out. 'We should have realized then. Sheltie always knows whether or not people are nice.'

Sheltie gave a loud snort, as if to say they should have listened to him in the first place.

'I know we should have trusted you, Sheltie,' said Emma. She threw her arms round his furry neck and kissed him on the nose. 'We'll stand guard over this one until the next flower comes up!' she said.

Dad laughed. 'I think you'd have to wait a long time, Emma,' he said. 'But perhaps the photo will do. We'll mark the spot so that the experts will know where to look.'

Sheltie gave a sudden snort and shook his head from side to side.

They heard footsteps.

Dave and Jim had come back. They didn't look as friendly as before.

'Sorry, sir, but we'll have to ask you to leave the site now,' said Dave, waving his mobile phone about. 'We've had orders from the boss.'

'What do you mean?' said Emma rudely. 'We've always come to Hawthorn Copse. You can't stop us. Not until you knock it down.'

'Just a minute, Emma,' said Dad gently. He turned to the men. 'Can you explain?'

'We let the little girls have their picnic

here yesterday because they didn't seem
to be doing any harm,' said Dave.

'And we didn't mind you coming to
look for your flower,' said Jim. 'But now
you know there isn't any rare flower,
you've got to leave. This is private land
now.'

'But there *is* a rare flower,' said Sally.
'We've got the photograph to prove it.'

131

'Who says you took the photo here?' said Jim with an unpleasant smile. 'It's your word against ours. Nobody's going to believe a school kid.'

'Anyway, our company checked the land,' said Dave. 'They know there isn't anything important here.'

Sheltie suddenly gave a loud whinny and pushed against Emma.

'I think Sheltie's on to something,' said Emma. 'Let's follow him.'

The little pony walked further into the wood and stopped by a bank of soft grass. He lifted his head and whickered, then bent down again, as if he wanted Emma to look at the bank.

They all looked down. Just peeping up through the grass were the heads of two more Military orchids!

'Sheltie, you're a genius!' said Dad. 'Sally, take lots of photos. Start from a distance away and then move in so that we can prove that this is the place we found them.'

'Where *Sheltie* found them!' said Emma proudly.

But the two surveyors began to behave in a very unpleasant way.

'You've got to move off this site,' shouted Dave. 'We'll call the police if necessary.'

'I'm sorry, but you'll have to take notice now,' said Dad. 'The council may well want to withdraw planning permission for your houses because this flower is protected. I think *I'll* call the police.' He took his mobile phone out of his pocket and rapidly tapped in the number of Little Applewood police station. He spoke quickly into the phone and then smiled at the men.

'PC Green will be here in a few minutes,' he said.

Lots of experts came to look at the flowers over the next few days, and everyone agreed that it really was the very rare Military orchid. The two surveyors told the police that they never knew that the flower was so rare, and that they were only doing their job. The council decided that all development plans should be stopped without delay. Hawthorn Copse had been saved!

A group of flower experts even came to Emma's cottage to see Sheltie.

'We owe him more than just a thank

you!' said a red-haired young woman in dungarees. She handed a big bag to Emma. 'We rang your parents to find out what Sheltie would like most, so we've brought these carrots and apples.'

Sheltie came to the paddock gate, curious to see who these friends of Emma were.

'It's a present for you, Sheltie,' said Emma. 'But you mustn't have them all at once. I'll look after them for you.'

Sheltie reached his head over the gate and snatched the bag from Emma. He backed away, just out of reach, and looked at her with a mischievous sparkle in his eye. Then he turned and raced to the other side of the paddock, scattering apples and carrots as he went.

'Sheltie! Come back!' shouted Emma.
She climbed over the gate and went
running after him.

Sheltie waited for Emma to come up
to him, then, with a flick of his tail,
raced off again. Emma picked up a few
of the spilled apples, then panted back
to the gate to talk to the visitors.

'I can see that he may be a bit of a handful,' said the red-haired woman, 'but that's a wonderful pony you've got there!'